Disney

SPLASHTACULAR

CARTOON TALES

ADAPTED BY SCOTT PETERSON

Disney
PRESS

New York

Printed in Singapore
First Edition
1 3 5 7 9 10 8 6 4 2
Library of Congress Catalog Card Number: 2004112610

ISBN 0-7868-3610-5

For more Disney Press fun, visit www.disneybooks.com

CONTENTS

Disney · PIXAR

FINDING NEMO

THIS IS A STORY ABOUT LOVE, LOSS, ADVENTURE, AND, OF COURSE, FISH. MEET MARLIN AND CORAL. THEY'RE GETTING READY FOR THEIR NEW EGGS TO HATCH.

WE HAVE TO NAME THEM. I LIKE NEMO.

NEMO? WELL, WE'LL NAME ONE NEMO—

ALL OF THEM?!

—BUT I'D LIKE THE REST TO BE NAMED MARLIN JUNIOR.

SURE! THEY— OH, NO!

IT'S JUST YOU AND ME NOW. AND I PROMISE I'LL NEVER LET ANYTHING HAPPEN TO YOU . . . NEMO.

SUDDENLY, A BARRACUDA APPEARED AND BEGAN TO ATTACK! MARLIN TRIED TO SAVE THE EGGS, AND CORAL, BUT IT WAS NO USE. HE COULD ONLY SAVE ONE.

EVEN WHEN SAD THINGS HAPPEN, TIME MOVES ON. AND BEFORE MARLIN KNEW IT, NEMO WAS SIX YEARS OLD.

FIRST DAY OF SCHOOL!

NEMO!

YOU OKAY? YOU DON'T **NEED** TO GO TO SCHOOL, YOU KNOW. REMEMBER, THE OCEAN'S NOT A SAFE PLACE.

DAD! COME ON, OR WE'LL BE LATE.

SOONER THAN MARLIN WOULD HAVE LIKED, THEY WERE AT THE SCHOOL.

MR. RAY WAS BOLD AND EXCITING—EVERYTHING NEMO THOUGHT HIS DAD WASN'T.

THE DROP-OFF WAS THE ONE PLACE MARLIN HAD ALWAYS TOLD NEMO HE MUST NEVER, EVER GO—THE PLACE WHERE THE OPEN OCEAN BEGAN!

MARLIN HAD COME TO STOP NEMO FROM SWIMMING OUT INTO THE OCEAN. BUT NEMO GOT UPSET AND SWAM OUT TO SEA TO PROVE HE WAS BRAVE ENOUGH.

MARLIN WAS VERY SCARED. HE COULD DO NOTHING TO SAVE NEMO FROM THE DIVER. THE DIVER PUT NEMO IN A BAG AND TOOK HIM TO A BOAT.

AAAAAH!!!

BRUCE SMELLED BLOOD. AND THAT MADE HIM *HUNGRY*.
MARLIN AND DORY HIGHTAILED IT OUT OF THERE!

AND, MEANWHILE, NEMO HAD FOUND HIMSELF IN A NEW HOME . . .

BUBBLES! BUBBLES! MY BUBBLES!

AAH!

SLOW DOWN, LITTLE FELLA.

AW, HE'S SCARED.

I WANNA GO HOME. WHERE'S MY DAD?

PROBABLY BACK AT THE PET STORE.

BUT I'M FROM THE OCEAN.

HE HASN'T BEEN DECONTAMINATED YET! JACQUES!

VOILÀ. AND HE IS CLEAN.

IF THERE'S ANYTHING ELSE YOU NEED, HON, JUST ASK.

WELL, MAYBE NOT EXACTLY HOME. BUT NEMO COULD HAVE BEEN IN WORSE PLACES.

25

AFTER HE CHASED NIGEL AWAY, THE DENTIST LEANED DOWN TO TALK TO NEMO.

HEY, LITTLE GUY. THIS IS DARLA, MY NIECE. YOU'RE GONNA BE HER BIRTHDAY PRESENT ON FRIDAY.

NOT DARLA!

WHAT'S WRONG WITH HER?

SEE THAT PICTURE? SHE'S A FISH KILLER!

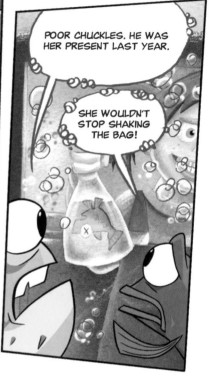

POOR CHUCKLES. HE WAS HER PRESENT LAST YEAR.

SHE WOULDN'T STOP SHAKING THE BAG!

I CAN'T GO WITH THAT GIRL! I HAVE TO GET BACK TO MY DAD! HE DOESN'T KNOW WHERE I AM AND— HEY!

NEMO FELT A STRONG SUCTION PULLING ON HIM—IT WAS THE WATER FILTER!

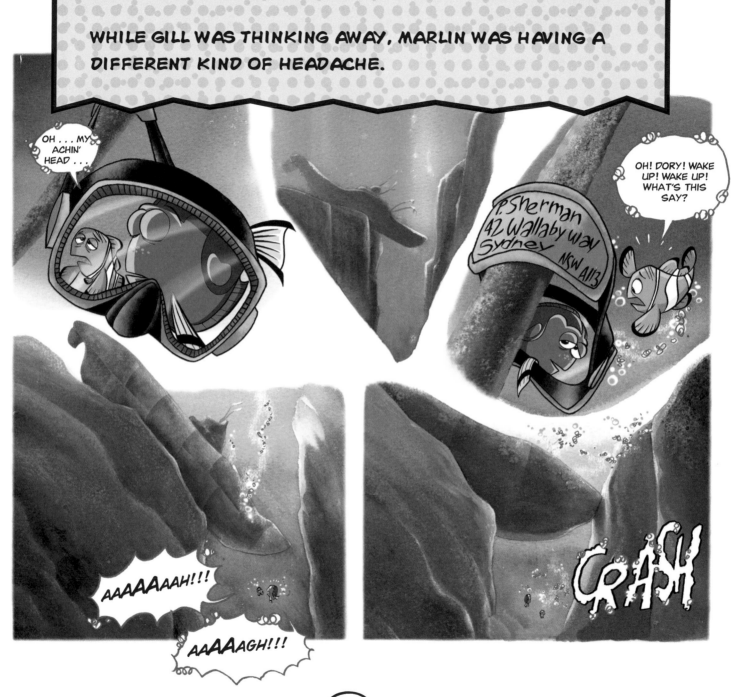

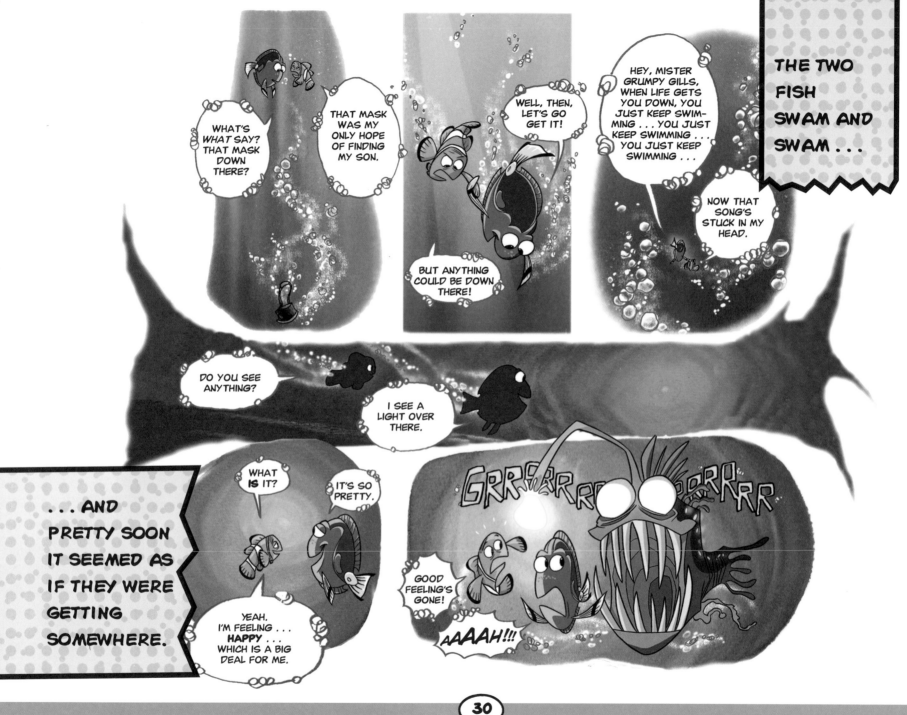

MARLIN WAS HAVING A LITTLE TROUBLE PUTTING UP WITH DORY. ESPECIALLY NOW THAT HE WAS BEING CHASED BY A HUGE ANGLERFISH! BUT HE GRABBED THE LIGHT AND HELD IT FOR DORY.

BACK IN NEMO'S NEW TANK, GILL WAS GETTING READY TO PUT HIS PLAN INTO ACTION.

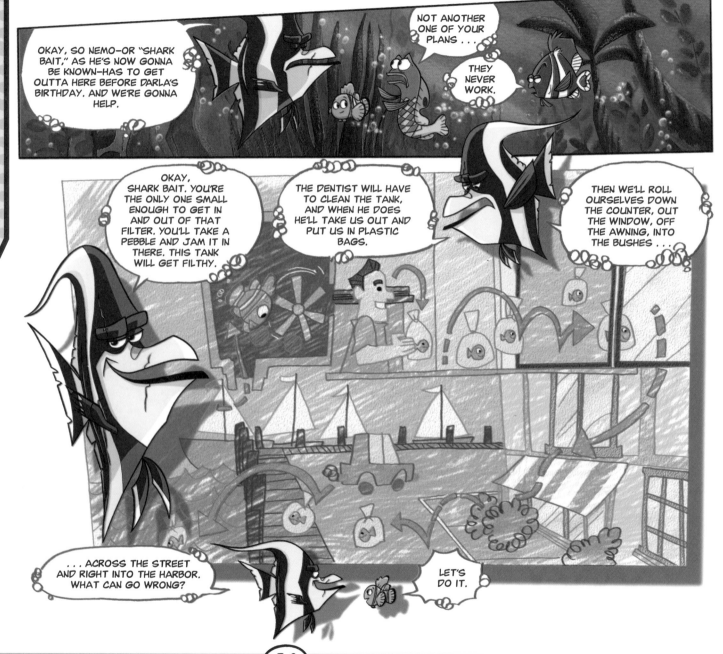

OKAY, SO NEMO—OR "SHARK BAIT," AS HE'S NOW GONNA BE KNOWN—HAS TO GET OUTTA HERE BEFORE DARLA'S BIRTHDAY. AND WE'RE GONNA HELP.

NOT ANOTHER ONE OF YOUR PLANS . . .

THEY NEVER WORK.

OKAY, SHARK BAIT. YOU'RE THE ONLY ONE SMALL ENOUGH TO GET IN AND OUT OF THAT FILTER. YOU'LL TAKE A PEBBLE AND JAM IT IN THERE. THIS TANK WILL GET FILTHY.

THE DENTIST WILL HAVE TO CLEAN THE TANK, AND WHEN HE DOES HE'LL TAKE US OUT AND PUT US IN PLASTIC BAGS.

THEN WE'LL ROLL OURSELVES DOWN THE COUNTER, OUT THE WINDOW, OFF THE AWNING, INTO THE BUSHES . . .

. . . ACROSS THE STREET AND RIGHT INTO THE HARBOR. WHAT CAN GO WRONG?

LET'S DO IT.

WHILE GILL WAS PLANNING THE FISH'S ESCAPE FROM THE DENTIST'S, MARLIN AND DORY WERE GETTING DIRECTIONS TO THE DENTIST'S OFFICE FROM A SCHOOL OF FISH.

TAKE THE EAC—THE EAST AUSTRALIAN CURRENT. IT'S THAT WAY.

HEY, THANKS, GUYS!

LET'S GO!

OH, AND WHEN YOU COME TO THE TRENCH, MAKE SURE YOU SWIM **OVER** IT, NOT **THROUGH** IT.

I'LL REMEMBER.

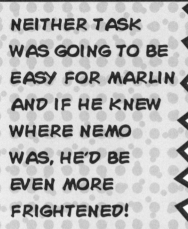

NEITHER TASK WAS GOING TO BE EASY FOR MARLIN AND IF HE KNEW WHERE NEMO WAS, HE'D BE EVEN MORE FRIGHTENED!

CHECKIN' OUT MY SCARS? THIS ONE'S FROM WHEN I LANDED ON THE DENTIST'S TOOLS—I WAS AIMIN' FOR THE TOILET.

WHY?

ALL DRAINS LEAD TO THE OCEAN, KID.

MISS YOUR DAD, DON'T YOU? YOU'RE LUCKY TO HAVE SOMEONE LOOKIN' FOR YA, SHARK BAIT.

HE'S NOT LOOKING FOR ME. HE'S SCARED OF THE OCEAN.

HMM. OKAY, HERE WE GO—THERE'S A GAP ABOVE THE WATER WHEEL JUST BIG ENOUGH FOR YOU TO LEAP THROUGH. THEN SWIM TO THE BOTTOM.

HEY, NICE JOB. HERE'S THE PEBBLE.

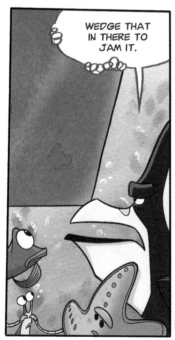

WEDGE THAT IN THERE TO JAM IT.

GILL! IT'S SUCKING ME BACK! HELP!

SHARK BAIT! GRAB HOLD OF THIS!

PULL!

IT'S OKAY, SHARK BAIT. YOU DID YOUR BEST.

AT SEA, MARLIN WAS TRYING TO HELP HIS HURT FRIEND. HE MET UP WITH A TURTLE NAMED CRUSH.

SO WHAT BRINGS YOU TO THE EAC?

WELL, DORY AND I— DORY! IS SHE—

SHE'S SUB-LEVEL.

OH, DORY. I'M SO SORRY. THIS IS ALL MY FAULT.

TWENTY-NINE, THIRTY! READY OR NOT, HERE I COME!

WHA-HUH?

YOU'D THINK BY NOW MARLIN WOULD EXPECT THE UNEXPECTED WITH DORY.

BUT DORY WAS STILL FULL OF SURPRISES.

CATCH ME IF YOU CAN!

AWESOME!

GASP!

THE YOUNG TURTLES LOVED TO TAKE RISKS, BUT WHEN MARLIN TRIED TO STOP THEM, CRUSH STOPPED HIM.

HANG ON THERE, DUDE. LET US SEE WHAT HAPPENS.

BUT ONE OF THEM MIGHT GET HURT!

HEY, DAD, DID YOU SEE THAT?

YOU SO TOTALLY ROCK, SQUIRT! OH, INTRO-JELLYMAN, OFFSPRING. OFFSPRING, JELLYMAN.

ISN'T IT AWESOME, JELLYMAN? WHEN THE LITTLE DUDES ARE JUST EGGS WE LEAVE 'EM ON THE BEACH TO HATCH, AND THEY FIND THEIR WAY BACK TO THE BIG OL' BLUE.

BUT HOW DO YOU KNOW WHEN THEY'RE READY?

WELL, YOU NEVER REALLY KNOW, BUT WHEN THEY KNOW, YOU'LL KNOW. YOU KNOW?

ALL RIGHT, EVERYONE— PIG PILE!

DID YOU REALLY TAKE ON THE JELLIES?

DID THEY STING?

DID YOU DIE?

WHERE YOU GOIN'?

WELL . . . IT'S LIKE THIS . . .

SEE, MY SON NEMO WAS TAKEN AWAY FROM ME.

NO WAY!

OOH . . .

THE WORD BEGAN TO GET OUT . . .

. . . SO THEY BUMP INTO THESE THREE HUGE SHARKS, RIGHT? BUT MARLIN SCARES THEM . . .

AND SLOWLY, THE TALE OF A FATHER'S UNSTOPPABLE QUEST TO FIND HIS ONLY SON . . .

AND THE STORY FINALLY MAKES ITS WAY *BEYOND* THE OCEAN.

KID! KID! YOUR DAD'S BEEN FIGHTIN' THE ENTIRE OCEAN LOOKIN' FOR YOU, TAKIN' ON SHARKS AND JELLYFISH! HE'S ON HIS WAY HERE NOW!

SEE, KID?!

MY DAD?

SHARK BAIT!

OH NO . . .

WE GOTTA GET HIM OUTTA THERE!

BUT THIS TIME NEMO *KNEW* HE COULD JAM THE FILTER WITH THE PEBBLE.

THERE WE GO!

YOU *DID* IT?

ALL RIGHT, SHARK BAIT! NOW, THIS TANK'S GONNA GET SO FILTHY THE DENTIST WILL **HAVE** TO CLEAN IT!

AS CRUSH SWAM AWAY, MARLIN AND DORY FOUND THEMSELVES FACING A BLANK WALL OF MURKY WATER.

SAY WHAT YOU WILL ABOUT BEING SWALLOWED BY A WHALE . . .

BUT IN THE DENTIST'S OFFICE, THINGS WEREN'T QUITE SO CLEAR. OR, RATHER, THEY *WERE*. AND THAT WAS A PROBLEM.

THE DENTIST MUST HAVE INSTALLED A NEW FILTER WHILE WE WERE SLEEPING.

OH NO! THE TANK'S CLEAN!

THE ESCAPE PLAN'S RUINED!

WHAT DO WE DO?

WHO'S THAT?

DARLA!

GASP!

GILL!

SWIM DOWN, KID!

GILL JUMPED IN TO HELP— A LITTLE TEAMWORK MAKES JUST ABOUT ANYTHING POSSIBLE.

WE CAN DO THIS! JUST SWIM DOWN!

HE'S GONNA MAKE IT!

YIKES!

TOGETHER GILL AND NEMO MANAGED TO SNAP THE NET. BUT THE DENTIST WASN'T GIVING UP THAT EASILY.

THERE WE GO. NOW WHERE'S THAT TRAY?

ROLL, KID! ROLL!

HOLD ON THERE—THAT'D BE A NASTY FALL.

THE DENTIST GRABBED NEMO, NOW HE'D NEVER GET OUT OF THE OFFICE AND BACK TO THE SEA.

NIGEL RUSHED THE FISH TO THE DENTIST'S OFFICE.

FROM NIGEL'S BILL, MARLIN SPOTTED NEMO, WHO LOOKED TO BE IN DEEP TROUBLE.

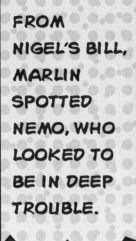

FISHY, FISHY, FISH—

EEEEEEE!!!

SMACK

WHAT'S GOING ON TODAAAAAY!

THUNK

THUD

WHOA!

GO ON, SHARK BAIT! TELL YOUR DAD WE SAID HEY.

WHOA!

WHEE!

WHOA.

NEMO WENT RIGHT DOWN THE DRAIN!

JUST THEN, NEMO POPPED OUT OF A NEARBY DRAIN! HE STARTED TO LOOK FOR HIS DAD AND SWAM INTO DORY.

HI . . . ARE YOU ALL RIGHT? YOU SEEM SAD.

I THINK I LOST SOMEBODY, BUT I CAN'T REMEMBER.

I'M LOOKING FOR SOMEONE TOO. WE CAN LOOK TOGETHER.

OH . . . THANK YOU. I'M DORY.

I'M NEMO.

NEMO. HUH. THAT'S A NICE NAME.

IT LOOKED LIKE DORY'S SHORT-TERM-MEMORY PROBLEM HAD RETURNED . . .

NEMO, NEMO. NEMO? NEMO! YOU'RE NEMO! YOUR FATHER ISN'T GONNA BELIEVE—OH, YOUR FATHER, YOUR FATHER!

YOU KNOW MY DAD? WHERE IS HE?

I THINK HE WENT THIS WAY. EXCUSE ME, HAVE YOU SEEN AN ORANGE FISH SWIM BY HERE?

YEAH, BUT I'M NOT TELLIN' YA WHICH WAY HE WENT, AND YOU CAN'T MAKE ME!

DORY LIFTED THE CRAB OUT OF THE WATER WHERE SOME REAL HUNGRY BIRDS WERE WAITING.

MINE! MINE!

I'LL TELL! I'LL TELL!

AND SO, THANKS TO ONE SUDDENLY VERY HELPFUL CRAB, NEMO AND DORY WERE SOON ON THEIR WAY.

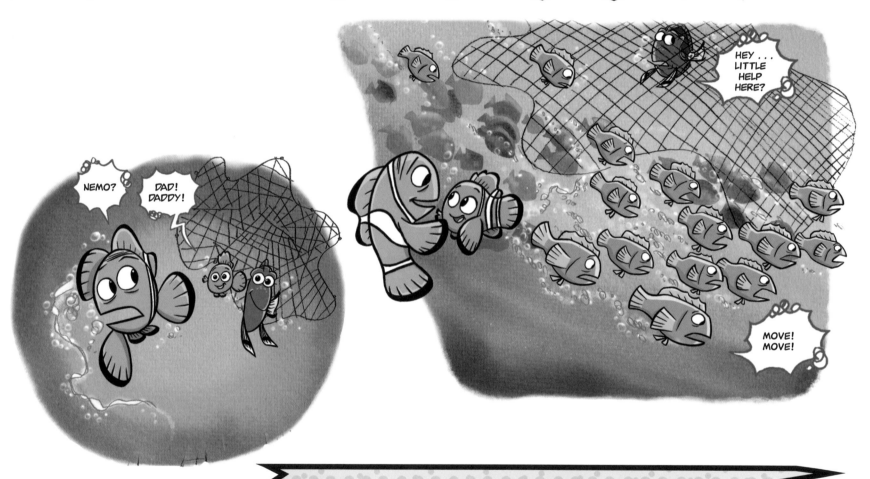

UNFORTUNATELY, WHEN IT COMES TO A FISHING NET . . .

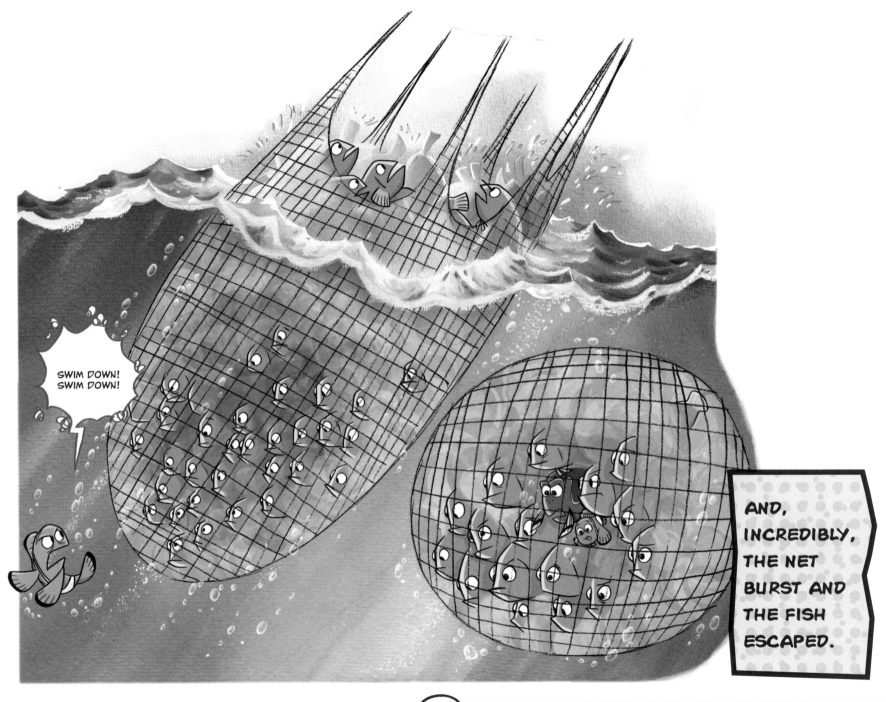

THINGS SEEMED TO BE JUST RIGHT AGAIN.

IN FACT, THEY WERE *BETTER* THAN *EVER*.

A FEW WEEKS AND A COUPLE THOUSAND MILES LATER . . .
I'M GONNA WIN!
NO YOU'RE NOT!
OH . . . YOU **JUST** BEAT ME!
YEAH, RIGHT!
WELL, WELCOME BACK, NEMO! AND WHO'S THIS?
EXCHANGE STUDENT.
I'M FROM THE EAC, DUDE!
AWESOME.

THE OTHER PARENTS WERE STILL TRYING TO WRAP THEIR HEADS AROUND THE IDEA THAT MARLIN, OF ALL FISH, WAS TRULY THE HERO THEY'D ALL HEARD ABOUT.

AND AS THE KIDS WERE HEADING OF TO SCHOOL . . .

SO, SERIOUSLY—DID YOU **REALLY** DO ALL THAT STUFF THEY SAY YOU DID?

WELL . . .

EXCUSE US.

JUST WANTED TO MAKE SURE OUR NEWEST MEMBER GOT HOME ALL RIGHT.

THANKS, GUYS!

GASP!

OH, MISTER RAY! WAIT! I FORGOT SOMETHING!

LOVE YOU, DAD.

I LOVE YOU TOO, NEMO.

ALL'S WELL THAT ENDS WELL.

Disney's THE LITTLE MERMAID

AS EVERY TRUE SAILOR KNOWS, DEEP BENEATH THE OCEAN'S WAVES LIVES A RARELY SEEN RACE OF PEOPLE: THE MERFOLK. THEY'RE RULED BY THE POWERFUL KING TRITON, FATHER TO SIX BEAUTIFUL DAUGHTERS, THE YOUNGEST OF WHOM IS ARIEL.

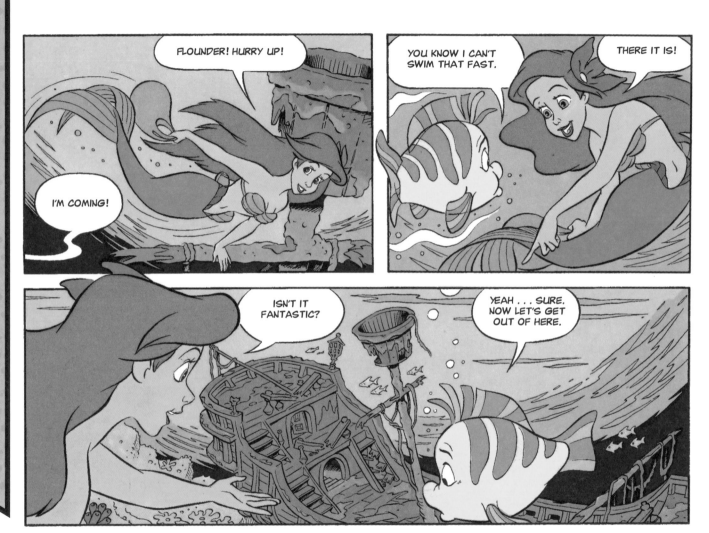

ARIEL WANTED TO CHECK OUT THE SHIPWRECK.
SHE DIDN'T WANT TO LEAVE.

HAVE YOU EVER SEEN ANYTHING SO WONDERFUL IN YOUR LIFE?

COOL.

BUT WHAT IS IT?

I DON'T KNOW.

BUT I BET SCUTTLE WILL!

I WONDER WHAT **THIS** IS.

YOU HEAR SOMETHING?

SHARK!

CRASH

REALIZING THEY WERE IN DEEP TROUBLE, ARIEL AND FLOUNDER SWAM AWAY QUICKLY. THEN THEY WENT TO SEE THE WORLD'S LEADING EXPERT ON HUMAN ARTIFACTS.

OR, MORE ACCURATELY, THEY WENT TO SEE THE ONLY CREATURE THEY KNEW WHO HAD EVEN THE SLIGHTEST *IDEA* ABOUT PEOPLE STUFF—THEIR FRIEND SCUTTLE.

THIS IS SPECIAL—IT'S A DINGLEHOPPER!

WOW!

HUMANS USE THESE TO STRAIGHTEN THEIR HAIR—JUST A TWIRL HERE AND A YANK THERE, AND YOU'VE GOT A PLEASING CONFIGURATION OF HAIR.

WHAT ABOUT THAT?

THIS IS A BANDED, BULBOUS SNARFBLATT! IT DATES BACK TO PREHYSTERICAL TIMES . . .

. . . AND MAKES THE MOST BEAUTIFUL—

—MUSIC.

MUSIC?

MUSIC! ARIEL SUDDENLY REMEMBERED SHE HAD AN APPOINTMENT.

SEE, THERE WAS THIS HUGE CONCERT SHE WAS SUPPOSED TO SING AT FOR ALL THE MERPEOPLE. AND, UH . . . WELL, SHE'D BEEN EXPLORING SUNKEN SHIPS INSTEAD. HER DAD WAS *NOT* GOING TO BE PLEASED. BUT THERE WAS SOMEONE *ELSE* WHO WAS VERY PLEASED WITH ARIEL'S ACTIONS ON THIS DAY . . .

. . . THE EVIL SEA-WITCH URSULA— KING TRITON'S GREATEST ENEMY.

AT THAT MOMENT, HOWEVER, KING TRITON WAS PRIMARILY CONCERNED WITH HOW TO GET HIS BELOVED DAUGHTER TO BEHAVE LIKE A GOOD PRINCESS.

BECAUSE OF YOUR CARELESSNESS, THE ENTIRE CELEBRATION WAS COMPLETELY RUINED!

COMPLETELY RUINED!

WHAT HAVE YOU TO SAY FOR YOURSELF?

I'LL TELL YOU WHAT THERE IS TO SAY—I'M A LAUGHING STOCK, THANKS TO YOU!

IT'S NOT HER FAULT!

FIRST THIS SHARK CHASED US . . .

SO WE TRIED TO . . . BUT THEN HE . . . UNTIL WE WERE SAFE . . .

AND THE SEAGULL WOULDN'T STOP TALKING—

SEAGULL?

DO YOU MEAN TO TELL ME YOU WENT UP TO THE SURFACE AGAIN?

WHOOPS. ARIEL WAS IN T-R-O-U-B-L-E.

75

THAT'LL TEACH A CRAB NOT TO SHOOT OFF HIS MOUTH TO ROYALTY.

SEBASTIAN HAD NEVER SEEN SO MANY HUMAN THINGS BEFORE. FOR THAT MATTER, NEITHER HAD ANYONE ELSE UNDER THE SEA, OTHER THAN ARIEL AND FLOUNDER.

ARIEL . . . WHAT ARE YOU . . . HOW COULD YOU . . . IF YOUR FATHER KNEW ABOUT ALL THIS!

YOU'RE NOT GONNA TELL HIM, ARE YOU?

YOU'RE UNDER A LOT PRESSURE DOWN HERE, ARIEL. I'LL TAKE YOU HOME AND GET YOU SOMETHING WARM TO DRINK AND—

DID YOU HEAR THAT?

WHAT DO YOU SUPPOSE *THAT* IS?

SEBASTIAN GOT THE FEELING THAT ARIEL WASN'T QUITE AS INTERESTED IN HIS PLAN AS HE WAS.

JUST THEN, SCUTTLE FLEW BY . . .

HEY THERE, SWEETIE! QUITE A SHOW, HUH?

I'VE NEVER SEEN A HUMAN THIS CLOSE BEFORE.

HE'S VERY HANDSOME, ISN'T HE?

WOOF!

I DON'T KNOW.

HE LOOKS KINDA HAIRY TO ME.

NOT THAT ONE. THE ONE PLAYING THE SNARFBLATT.

SILENCE!

IT IS NOW MY HONOR AND PRIVILEGE TO PRESENT OUR ESTEEMED PRINCE ERIC . . .

FEW OF EVEN THESE EXPERT SAILORS HAD EVER SEEN A STORM QUITE LIKE THIS.

BUT PRINCE ERIC NEVER WAVERED, AND HIS COURAGE WAS AN INSPIRATION TO THEM ALL.

LOOK OUT!

OH NO!

BUT EVEN COURAGE CAN'T KEEP A SHIP OFF THE ROCKS.

THE SAILORS HAD NO CHOICE BUT TO ABANDON SHIP. ERIC'S DOG, MAX, WAS TOO TERRIFIED TO MOVE. ERIC HAD TO CARRY HIM TO SAFETY BEFORE THE FIRE HIT THE GUNPOWDER DOWN BELOW.

IT'S OKAY, MAX . . .

I'VE GOT— WHOA!

BAWR!

BOOM

ERIC!

ERIC DIDN'T MAKE IT IN TIME.

ARIEL KNEW SHE HAD ONLY SECONDS TO SAVE THE PRINCE SHE'D NEVER EVEN MET.

EXHAUSTED BY THE ENTIRE ORDEAL, ARIEL WAS AFRAID ALL HER EFFORTS HAD BEEN FOR NOTHING.

SCUTTLE . . . IS . . . IS HE–?

IT'S HARD TO SAY WITH HUMANS.

UH . . .

OH! HE IS BREATHING!

HE'S SO BEAUTIFUL.

I WOULD LOVE TO LIVE WHERE YOU LIVE.

ERIC?

HMM?

ERIC!

THE PRINCE KNEW HE WASN'T DREAMING . . . AND YET . . . HE FELT LIKE HE MUST HAVE BEEN.

THERE COULDN'T POSSIBLY BE ANYONE IN THE WORLD THAT BEAUTIFUL . . . OR WITH A VOICE THAT SWEET. BUT IF SHE WAS REAL . . . ERIC KNEW SHE WAS THE GIRL HE WOULD MARRY.

OH, ERIC—YOU DELIGHT IN THESE SADISTIC STRAINS ON MY BLOOD PRESSURE, DON'T YOU?

A GIRL . . . SHE RESCUED ME.

SHE WAS SINGING WITH THE MOST BEAUTIFUL VOICE.

I THINK YOU'VE SWALLOWED TOO MUCH SEAWATER.

COME, MAX.

WOOF!

THE SEA KING MUST NEVER KNOW ABOUT ALL THIS.

♪ SOMEDAY I'LL JOIN YOU IN YOUR WORLD. ♪

BUT WHILE ARIEL REJOICED, SOMEONE VERY, VERY POWERFUL ...AND VERY, VERY WICKED WAS BREWING A NASTY PLAN.

I CAN'T STAND IT! IT'S TOO EASY!

THE CHILD IS IN LOVE WITH A HUMAN! AND NOT JUST ANY HUMAN—A PRINCE!

KING TRITON'S HEADSTRONG LITTLE GIRL WILL MAKE A CHARMING ADDITION TO MY LITTLE GARDEN.

I'VE GOT TO SEE HIM AGAIN. TONIGHT! SCUTTLE KNOWS WHERE HE LIVES.

ARIEL!

GET YOUR HEAD OUT OF THE CLOUDS AND BACK IN THE WATER.

DOWN HERE IS YOUR HOME.

THE HUMAN WORLD IS A MESS.

LIFE UNDER THE SEA IS SO MUCH BETTER THAN ANYTHING THEY'VE GOT UP THERE.

OH, YEAH, WE'RE HAPPY DOWN IN THE MUCK HERE. AREN'T WE, ARIEL?

ARIEL AND FLOUNDER SWAM AWAY FROM SEBASTIAN.

AND FLOUNDER SHOWED ARIEL A VERY SPECIAL GIFT HE HAD FOR HER.

WHEN KING TRITON HAD HEARD THAT ARIEL MIGHT BE IN LOVE, THIS WAS *NOT* WHAT HE HAD EXPECTED.

OH . . .

POOR CHILD.

POOR, SWEET CHILD. SHE HAS A VERY SERIOUS PROBLEM.

BUT WE COULD HELP.

WHO . . . WHO ARE YOU?

DON'T BE SCARED. WE REPRESENT SOMEONE WHO CAN MAKE ALL YOUR DREAMS COME TRUE.

JUST IMAGINE, YOU AND YOUR PRINCE, TOGETHER FOREVER.

URSULA HAS GREAT POWERS.

THE SEA WITCH?!

I COULDN'T—NO! GET OUT OF HERE!

ARIEL HAD HEARD MANY TALES OF URSULA—ALL OF THEM BAD.

BUT LOVE AND ANGER CAN MAKE A MERMAID DO CRAZY THINGS.

SUIT YOURSELF.

WAIT.

YES?

I DIDN'T MEAN TO TELL THE SEA KING. IT WAS AN ACCIDENT. I . . . ARIEL?

WHERE ARE YOU GOING?

TO SEE URSULA. WHY DON'T YOU GO TATTLE TO MY FATHER? YOU'RE GOOD AT THAT.

A MOMENT BEFORE, SEBASTIAN HAD THOUGHT HE COULDN'T POSSIBLY FEEL ANY WORSE. NOW HE KNEW BETTER.

SOON, ARIEL ARRIVED AT THE CASTLE OF THE SEA WITCH.

COME IN.

OH!

OH!

WE MUSTN'T LURK IN DOORWAYS.

HMM?

SO, BECOMING HUMAN WAS URSULA'S IDEA OF "SIMPLE," HUH?

HERE'S THE DEAL—I'LL MAKE A POTION THAT WILL TURN YOU HUMAN FOR THREE DAYS.

BEFORE THE SUN SETS ON THE THIRD DAY, YOU'VE GOT TO GET OLD PRINCIE TO FALL IN LOVE WITH YOU.

THAT IS, HE'S GOT TO KISS YOU. AND NOT JUST ANY KISS—THE KISS OF TRUE LOVE.

IF HE DOES, YOU GET TO STAY HUMAN FOREVER.

BUT IF NOT, YOU TURN BACK INTO A MERMAID . . . AND YOU BELONG TO ME.

NO!

ARIEL'S FRIENDS PROTESTED. BUT IT WAS TOO LATE. THE DEED WAS SIGNED.

BUT ONCE SHE REACHED THE SURFACE, ARIEL FORGOT ALL ABOUT NEARLY DROWNING. SHE HAD *LEGS!*

ARIEL!

HEY, THERE'S SOMETHING DIFFERENT ABOUT YOU.

SHE'S GOT LEGS! GEEZ!

SEE, ARIEL'S GOT TO MAKE THE PRINCE FALL IN LOVE WITH HER IN THREE DAYS, SO SHE TRADED HER VOICE TO THE SEA WITCH FOR LEGS.

WELL, FIRST OF ALL, WE GOTTA DRESS YOU LIKE A HUMAN.

NOW **THAT'S** WHAT I'M TALKIN' ABOUT!

MAX?

OH!

ERIC TOOK ARIEL BACK TO HIS CASTLE. THE SERVANTS CLEANED AND GROOMED HER THERE.

MY GOODNESS, ISN'T SHE A VISION, ERIC?

A DINGLEHOPPER!

IT'S NOT OFTEN WE HAVE SUCH A LOVELY GUEST, IS IT, ERIC?

ARIEL THOUGHT SHE KNEW HOW TO USE A FORK. SCUTTLE HAD TOLD HER IT WAS FOR HER HAIR. AND NOW SHE WAS DOING JUST WHAT SCUTTLE HAD TOLD HER TO WITH IT.

ERIC THOUGHT ARIEL WAS STRANGE. BUT HE QUICKLY FOUND HIMSELF FALLING DEEPLY IN LOVE WITH THIS ODD GIRL.

JEEZ! WE'RE RUNNING OUT OF TIME HERE! KISS HER ALREADY!

COME ON! KISS HER!

YOU HEAR SOMETHING?

YOU KNOW, I FEEL BAD NOT KNOWING YOUR NAME. LET ME SEE—MILDRED? DIANA? RACHEL?

ARIEL! HER NAME IS ARIEL!

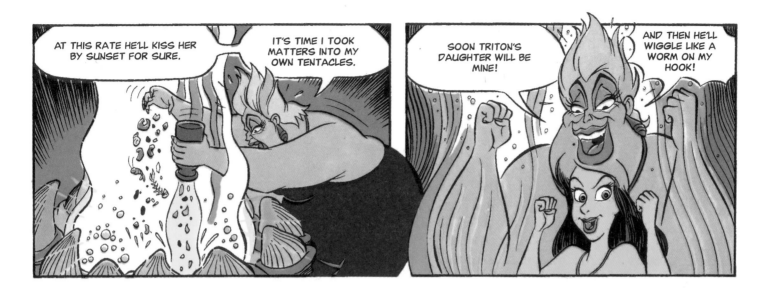

AFTER A MAGICAL TWO DAYS TOGETHER, PRINCE ERIC WAS FALLING DEEPLY IN LOVE WITH HIS MYSTERIOUS NEW FRIEND. YET HE JUST COULD NOT FORGET THE GIRL WHO HAD SAVED HIM FROM DROWNING . . . THE GIRL WITH THE INCREDIBLE VOICE . . .

THAT VOICE WAS ARIEL'S! URSULA HAD STOLEN IT AND HYPNOTIZED ERIC WITH IT!

WELL, ERIC, IT APPEARS I WAS MISTAKEN. THIS MYSTERY MAIDEN OF YOURS DOES, IN FACT, EXIST.

AND SHE CERTAINLY IS LOVELY.

WE WISH TO MARRIED RIGHT AWAY.

BUT . . . THESE THINGS TAKE TIME!

NO. THIS AFTERNOON.

THE WEDDING SHIP DEPARTS AT SUNSET.

VERY WELL, ERIC. AS YOU WISH.

ARIEL'S HEART WAS BROKEN.

SCUTTLE WAS CONFUSED. HE KNEW ARIEL HAD LOST HER VOICE.
HE KNEW THAT THIS WAS ARIEL'S VOICE HE WAS HEARING.
AND HE KNEW THAT IT *WASN'T* ARIEL HE WAS LOOKING AT.

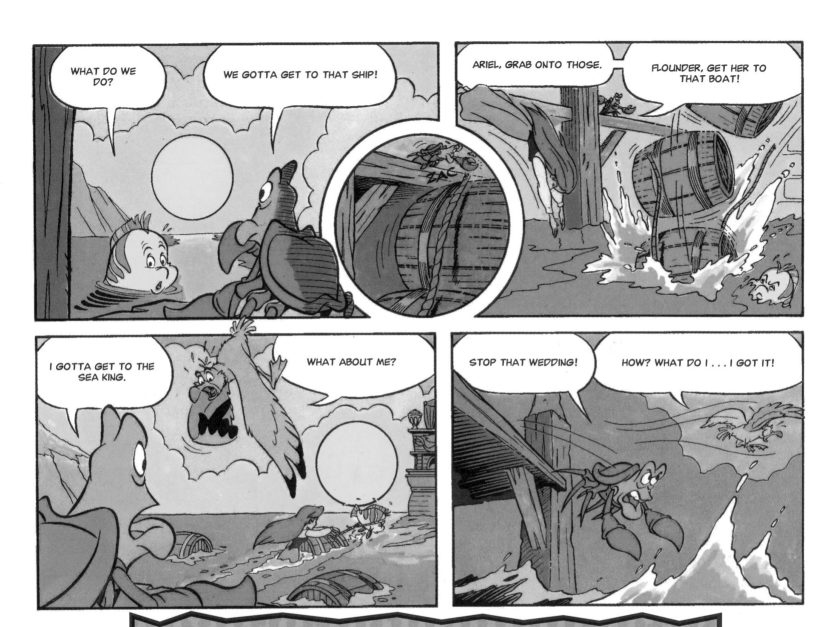

NORMALLY, OF COURSE, PUTTING SCUTTLE IN CHARGE OF SOMETHING SO IMPORTANT WOULD BE A TERRIBLE IDEA.

THE SEA WITCH DIDN'T TAKE THAT KIND OF THING WITHOUT A FIGHT, OF COURSE.

YOU LITTLE—

ERP.

AH!

SNAP

CRASH

ARIEL?

ARIEL HAD HER VOICE BACK!

BUT TRUE LOVE ISN'T ALWAYS ON TIME.

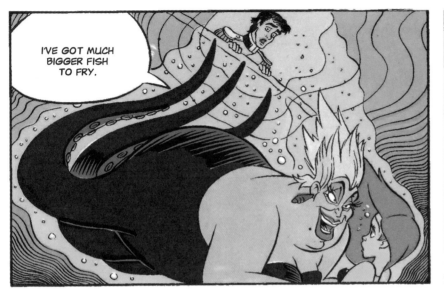

THE SEA KING WAS MIGHTY BIG AND POWERFUL . . .

THIS CONTRACT IS LEGAL AND COMPLETELY UNBREAKABLE!

OF COURSE . . . I ALWAYS HAD AN EYE FOR A BARGAIN. I WILL TRADE THE DAUGHTER OF THE SEA KING . . . FOR SOMEONE EVEN BETTER.

ERIC! WHAT ARE YOU DOING?

I'M NOT LOSING HER AGAIN!

DO WE HAVE A DEAL?

UNFORTUNATELY, WITH THE ADDITIONAL POWERS THE SEA WITCH GAINED UPON BECOMING THE SEA QUEEN . . .

WITH ONE WAVE OF HER WAND, URSULA CREATED A WHIRLPOOL THE LIKES OF WHICH THE OCEAN HAD NEVER BEFORE SEEN.

ERIC HAD MANAGED TO DEFEAT URSULA!

AND JUST LIKE THAT, URSULA WAS GONE, AND THE TRAPPED MERPEOPLE WERE FREE ONCE MORE.

WITH ONE PASS OF HER FATHER'S TRIDENT . . .

...ALL ARIEL'S DREAMS CAME TRUE AT LAST.

MY . . . FINS? THEY'RE CHANGING!

AND WITH HER BRAND-NEW LEGS, ARIEL DID WHAT SHE'D ALWAYS LONGED TO DO—RUN STRAIGHT INTO THE ARMS OF HER BELOVED.

WHO DOESN'T?

KING TRITON AND PRINCE ERIC BOWED TO EACH OTHER, A SIGN OF RESPECT AND GRATITUDE BETWEEN THE TWO PEOPLE WHO LOVED ARIEL MOST IN THE ENTIRE WORLD.

AND THE SEA KING ADDED ONE FINAL TOUCH TO THE PERFECT DAY . . .

Disney's

ATLANTIS

THE LOST EMPIRE

FRIGHTENED SOLDIERS WERE HELPING PEOPLE RUN FROM A TIDAL WAVE. AND THE PEOPLE WERE RUNNING VERY, VERY QUICKLY.

KIDA WATCHED HER MOTHER RISE UP AND DISAPPEAR. AND ALL THAT WAS LEFT WERE THE STONE GIANTS, THE PROTECTORS OF HER CITY.

THEN THEY, TOO, WERE SWALLOWED BY THE WATERS. AND THAT WAS THE END OF ATLANTIS.

THWMOSSSHHH

OR SO THEY THOUGHT FOR THOUSANDS OF YEARS. AND THEN, ONE DAY, MILO THATCH GOT READY TO PERSUADE A MUSEUM TO PAY FOR AN EXPEDITION. IT WAS A MISSION HIS GRANDFATHER HAD ALWAYS DREAMT OF....

GENTLEMEN, WE'VE ALL HEARD OF THE LEGEND OF ATLANTIS, A CONTINENT THAT WAS HOME TO AN ADVANCED CIVILIZATION WITH TECHNOLOGY AND A POWER SOURCE FAR BEYOND OUR OWN.

NOW, *THE SHEPHERD'S JOURNAL* IS A BOOK WHICH IS SAID TO BE A FIRST-HAND ACCOUNT OF ATLANTIS AND ITS LOCATION—WHICH I BELIEVE IS OFF THE COAST OF ICELAND.

RRRINNNG

CLICK

OOPS! TIME FOR MY REAL MEETING.

AS YOU MAY HAVE GUESSED, MILO DID *NOT* PERSUADE THE MUSEUM BOARD TO GIVE HIM MONEY.

DON'T WORRY. MISTER WHITMORE DOESN'T BITE . . . OFTEN.

HEY . . . THAT PICTURE . . . THAT'S MY—

YOUR GRANDFATHER.

FINEST MAN I EVER KNEW.

I'M PRESTON WHITMORE.

DID YOU REALLY KNOW MY GRANDFATHER?

SURE DID. THADDEUS WAS MY BEST FRIEND FOR MORE THAN FIFTY YEARS.

SO, WHY DID YOU COME TO FIND ME?

BECAUSE HE LEFT THAT BOOK BEHIND FOR YOU.

IT'S WRITTEN IN A LANGUAGE THAT NO LONGER EXISTS. BUT **I** CAN READ IT. AND IT PROVES MY GRANDFATHER WAS **RIGHT**.

WELL, THEN, I GUESS WE'D BEST GO FIND ATLANTIS.

CLICK

I PROMISED YOUR GRANDFATHER THAT IF THAT JOURNAL EVER WAS DISCOVERED, I'D FUND THE EXPEDITION TO ATLANTIS. HE'S GONE—BUT YOU'RE HERE.

IS THAT SHIP—?

FWEENNN... CLICK...TWICK

—THE ONE THAT'S GOING TO TAKE YOU TO DISCOVER ATLANTIS? YUP. AND THAT'S YOUR CREW. BRING ME PROOF, MILO. PROVE YOUR GRANDPA RIGHT.

I'M YOUR MAN, MISTER WHITMORE.

YOU HAVE DISTURBED THE DIRT!

EXCUSE ME?

DIRT FROM AROUND THE GLOBE! SPANNING THE CENTURIES! WHAT HAVE YOU DONE?

YOU MUST LEAVE AT ONCE!

MOLE, WHAT HAVE I TOLD YOU ABOUT PLAYING NICE?

GET BACK! I'VE GOT SOAP AND I'M NOT AFRAID TO USE IT! BACK, FOUL CREATURE!

NAME'S JOSHUA SWEET. YOU ALREADY MET MOLE.

MILO THATCH.

"UNDIVIDED ATTENTION" WAS AN ENTIRELY NEW EXPERIENCE FOR MILO.

MILO'S AUDIENCE SEEMED SKEPTICAL. LUCKILY, AT THAT MOMENT THE MEETING WAS INTERRUPTED.

THE SOUND MISS PACKARD HAD PICKED UP GOT LOUDER AND LOUDER, UNTIL IT WAS UNBEARABLE! THEN THE WHOLE SUB SHOOK.

THE MONSTER PICKED UP THE SUBMARINE. THINGS WERE GOING FROM BAD TO TERRIBLE!

AND JUST WHEN IT SEEMED THINGS COULDN'T GET ANY WORSE, THE SHIP WAS HIT CLEAN THROUGH!

KA---OOM

SIR, THEY SAY WE'VE GOT LESS THAN FIVE MINUTES BEFORE WE'RE DEAD.

CAP'N, WE'RE HIT BAD!

EVERYBODY GRAB A SEAT AND BUCKLE IN!

LIEUTENANT, GET US OUT OF HERE.

I'M ON IT.

THE LIEUTENANT MANAGED TO GET THEM OUT OF THERE QUICKLY.

ONLY PART OF THE SHIP WAS SAVED.

WE STARTED THIS EXPEDITION WITH TWO HUNDRED OF THE FINEST MEN AND WOMEN I'VE EVER KNOWN. WE'RE ALL THAT'S LEFT. WE HAVE A CRISIS ON OUR HANDS, BUT WE ARE **GOING** TO FIND A WAY THROUGH BY WORKING TOGETHER.

MILO DID HIS BEST TO BE USEFUL.

YOU **DO** KNOW HOW TO DRIVE, RIGHT?

OF COURSE! YOU GOT YOUR STEERING AND YOUR GAS AND YOUR BRAKE . . . AND THIS FUNNY LITTLE THINGIE HERE . . .

MILO WENT ON, NOT GIVING ANYONE MUCH CONFIDENCE IN HIS ABILITIES.

RRROOOMWWW

WHOOPS. UPSIDE-DOWN. **THAT** WAY.

THIS WAS THE ADVENTURE MILO HAD DREAMED OF. AND HERE HE WAS—BUT HE WAS STILL AN OUTSIDER.

MILO WAS TERRIBLY LONELY...

...HIS ONLY REAL FRIEND WAS THE JOURNAL HE READ AND REREAD.

BUT HIS READING MADE HIM WANT TO EXPLORE EVEN MORE. AND EXPLORE HE DID!

WOW! LOOK AT THE SIZE OF THIS! IT'S GOT TO BE A MILE HIGH AT THE LEAST! IT MUST HAVE TAKEN HUNDREDS—NO, **THOUSANDS** OF YEARS TO CARVE THIS THING!

KAFWOOOOM

HEY, LOOK, I MADE A BRIDGE. AND IT ONLY TOOK ME, WHAT, TEN SECONDS—ELEVEN, TOPS.

THE CREW VENTURED OVER THE FALLEN COLUMN AND TOWARD ATLANTIS.

YOU KNOW, WE'VE BEEN PRETTY ROUGH ON THE KID. WHAT SAY WE CUT HIM SOME SLACK?

GOOD IDEA. HEY, MILO, WHY DON'T YOU COME SIT WITH US?

REALLY? YOU DON'T MIND?

DON'T YOU EVER STOP READING THAT BOOK?

THERE'S SOMETHING THAT JUST DOESN'T MAKE SENSE.

SEE, IN THIS PASSAGE, THE SHEPHERD SEEMS TO BE LEADING UP TO SOMETHING HE CALLS "THE HEART OF ATLANTIS"—COULD BE THE POWER SOURCE. BUT THEN IT JUST CUTS OFF.

KID, RELAX. WE DON'T GET PAID OVERTIME.

I KNOW, I GET CARRIED AWAY. BUT THAT'S WHAT THIS IS ALL ABOUT, RIGHT? DISCOVERY, ADVENTURE, TEAMWORK?

NOT EVERYONE AGREED.

THE REST OF THE TEAM THOUGHT THEIR QUEST WAS ABOUT SOMETHING ELSE ENTIRELY.

MONEY.

MONEY.

I'M GONNA SAY, MONEY.

MONEY.

MONEY.

OR MAYBE IT'S JUST THE MONEY.

SOMETHING WRONG WITH YOUR NECK?

YEAH, I HURT IT WHEN I–

YAARGH!

CRRRICK

THAT BETTER?

I . . . YEAH! WHERE'D YOU LEARN THAT?

ARAPAHOE MEDICINE MAN. GOT A SHEEPSKIN FROM HOWARD U. AND A BEARSKIN FROM OL' IRON CLOUD.

AIN'T YA GONNA PITCH YOUR TENT?

I, UH . . . I DID. GUESS I'M A LITTLE RUSTY. HAVEN'T BEEN CAMPING SINCE THE LAST TIME GRANDPA TOOK ME.

VINNY FIXED MILO'S TENT FOR HIM. AND WHILE HE DID, MILO GOT TO KNOW AUDREY A LITTLE BIT BETTER.

WHAT WAS YOUR GRANDFATHER LIKE?

HE WAS AMAZING. MY PARENTS DIED WHEN I WAS LITTLE, AND HE RAISED ME.

NO MATTER WHAT, HE ALWAYS HAD TIME FOR ME.

MY PARENTS WANTED SONS.

I'M HERE TO GET MONEY TO OPEN A GARAGE WITH MY DAD.

ME, I JUST LIKE TO BLOW THINGS UP. A LOT.

COME ON, VINNY—TELL THE TRUTH.

OKAY. ONE DAY, IN MY FAMILY'S FLOWER SHOP, THERE WAS THIS GAS LEAK. BOOM! BLEW ME RIGHT THROUGH THE WINDOW.

IT WAS A THING OF SUCH BEAUTY.

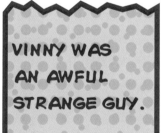

VINNY WAS AN AWFUL STRANGE GUY.

FOOM FAFOOM

ODD, GORGEOUS, AND VERY DANGEROUS FIREFLIES.

FIRE! FIRE!

THATCH... GO BACK...

GET SOME WATER ON THAT FIRE!

TOO LATE FOR THAT. INTO THOSE CAVES—MOVE, PEOPLE!

AND MERE MOMENTS LATER...

KABOOOOOOMM

AN EXPLOSION DESTROYED THE BRIDGE VINNY HAD CREATED.

THE CREW LOST ALMOST EVERYTHING THEY HAD BROUGHT.

SO WHO'S NOT DEAD YET? AUDREY, STATUS REPORT.

WELL, LOOKS LIKE WE'VE STILL GOT THE DIGGER. BUT WHERE'S MILO?

<HE'S DRESSED SO STRANGELY.>

<WHERE DID HE COME FROM?>

<HE MUST BE FROM THE SURFACE.>

ERGH.

<BUT HOW DID HE GET HERE?>

<SHOULD WE KILL HIM?>

MILO DIDN'T UNDERSTAND WHAT THEY WERE SAYING. THEY WERE SPEAKING ANOTHER LANGUAGE.

AND THEN MILO HAD HIS FIRST REAL LOOK AT THE MYSTERIOUS WOMAN WHO WAS CLEARLY IN CHARGE.

‹HE . . . HE DOESN'T APPEAR HOSTILE. JUST HURT.›

YOW!

HEY . . .

NO! WAIT! DON'T GO! PLEASE!

THEY DISAPPEARED SUDDENLY . . .

163

AND THEY HAD FOUND SOMETHING ELSE.

HOLY CATS. WHO ARE THESE GUYS?

GOTTA BE ATLANTEANS.

THAT'S IMPOSSIBLE!

SEEN THIS BACK IN DAKOTA. THEY CAN SMELL FEAR, SO BE QUIET.

<WHO ARE YOU AND WHERE DO YOU COME FROM?>

UM . . . WHO ARE YOU AND WHERE DO YOU COME FROM?

<YOUR MANNER OF SPEECH IS STRANGE TO ME.>

PARLEZ-VOUS FRANCAIS?

OUI, MONSIEUR!

IT'S HANDY TO SPEAK TWO DOZEN DIFFERENT LANGUAGES!

YOUR HEART HAS SOFTENED, KIDA. A THOUSAND YEARS AGO YOU WOULD HAVE SLAIN THEM.

THEN THE STREETS WERE LIT, AND OUR PEOPLE DID NOT HAVE TO SCAVENGE FOR FOOD. WE WERE GREAT ONCE.

OUR WAY OF LIFE IS PRESERVED. WHEN YOU TAKE THE THRONE, YOU WILL UNDERSTAND.

BUT IF THESE OUTSIDERS CAN UNLOCK THE SECRETS OF OUR PAST, WE CAN SAVE OUR FUTURE!

SO HOW'D IT GO?

EH. THE KING AND HIS DAUGHTER DON'T QUITE SEE EYE-TO-EYE. SHE SEEMS TO LIKE US OKAY, BUT THE KING . . . I THINK HE'S HIDING SOMETHING.

WHICH IS HOW MILO GOT "VOLUNTEERED" INTO GOING TO TALK TO KIDA THAT NIGHT.

IT IS SAID THAT THE GODS BECAME ANGRY WITH ATLANTIS AND SENT A GREAT CATACLYSM. ALL I REMEMBER IS THE SKY GOING DARK AND PEOPLE RUNNING, THEN A BRIGHT LIGHT FLOATING OVER THE CITY. MY FATHER SAID IT CALLED MY MOTHER TO IT. I NEVER SAW HER AGAIN.

YES.

WAIT A MINUTE. YOU WERE THERE? THAT MEANS YOU'RE 4,800 YEARS OLD!

OH. WELL, UH . . . LOOKIN' GOOD! SO DO **YOU** HAVE ANY QUESTIONS?

YES. HOW DID YOU FIND US?

MILO AND KIDA DECIDED TO TOUR THE CITY BY FOOT.

WOW.

WHAT IS WRONG?

IT'S JUST . . . MY GRANDPA USED TO TELL ME STORIES OF THIS PLACE AS LONG AS I CAN REMEMBER. I JUST . . . I JUST WISH HE WERE HERE.

MILO SUDDENLY REALIZED THAT ROURKE HAD STOLEN THE MISSING PAGE.

All Rourke cared about was stealing the crystal—even if it meant that all the Atlanteans would die.

WHAT DOES THE JOURNAL SAY ABOUT THE CRYSTAL?

JUST THAT "THE HEART OF ATLANTIS LIES IN THE EYES OF HER KING."

WELL, THEN, MAYBE OUR FRIEND HERE CAN HELP. WHERE'S THE CRYSTAL CHAMBER, CHIEF?

YOU WILL DESTROY US AND YOURSELVES.

I DON'T THINK YOU UNDERSTAND.

YOU WILL DIE FOR HURTING HIM

THUD.

THIS WAS NOT THE PLAN!

PLAN'S CHANGED, DOC. DIPLOMACY HAS FAILED, SO I'M GOING TO COUNT TO TEN AND YOU'RE GOING TO TELL ME WHERE THE CRYSTAL IS. ONE . . . TWO . . . NINE . . . TE-

"THE HEART OF ATLANTIS LIES IN THE EYES OF HER KING!" THIS IS IT!

JUST THEN, THE CHAMBER FLOODED WITH LIGHT. . . .

AND SHE ENTERED INTO THE HEART OF ATLANTIS.

KIDA!

DON'T TOUCH HER!

AND CAME DOWN . . . DIFFERENT.

AND THEN SHE GOT OUT OF THE TRUCK. AND SO DID VINNY. AND SWEET. AND COOKIE AND MOLE AND PACKARD.

WE'RE ALL GONNA DIE.

ROURKE, THIS IS WRONG.

YOU CANNOT BE SERIOUS. WELL, IF THAT'S THE WAY YOU WANT IT—MORE FOR ME.

WE CAN'T LET HIM DO THIS!

WAIT A SECOND.

JUST AFTER ROURKE'S TRUCK PASSED, THE BRIDGE EXPLODED.

KA-VOOOM

NOW YOU CAN GO.

MILO, YOU BETTER COME.

HE'S NOT DOING WELL—INTERNAL BLEEDING.

BUT THESE CRYSTALS HAVE SOME SORT OF HEALING ENERGY!

WHERE IS KIDA?

SHE . . . UH . . .

SHE HAS BEEN CHOSEN, LIKE HER MOTHER. IN TIMES OF DANGER, THE CRYSTAL CHOOSES A HOST TO PROTECT ITSELF AND ITS PEOPLE.

HOLD ON—CHOOSE? THIS THING IS **ALIVE?**

IT THRIVES ON THE EMOTIONS OF ALL WHO CAME BEFORE US. IN RETURN, IT PROVIDES POWER AND PROTECTION. AND AS IT GREW, IT DEVELOPED A CONSCIOUSNESS OF ITS OWN.

MILO, THE CREW, AND A FEW DOZEN ATLANTEANS ENDED UP FINDING ROURKE AND HELGA JUST BEFORE THEY MANAGED TO GET AWAY WITH KIDA.

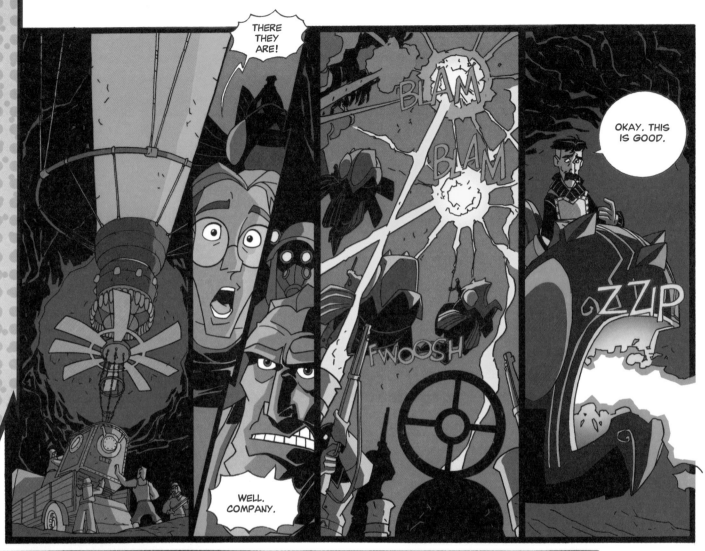

THERE THEY ARE!

WELL. COMPANY.

OKAY. THIS IS GOOD.

BLAM

BLAM

FWOOSH

ZZIP

ZZIP

VINNY! DON'T LET THEM REACH THE TOP!

DESPERATE TO SAVE KIDA AND ATLANTIS, MEEK, MILD-MANNERED MILO DID THE UNTHINKABLE— HE JUMPED OUT AND ATTACKED ROURKE.

HMM?

TUNK

YOU KNOW, MILO, YOU'RE A BIGGER PAIN THAN I WOULD EVER HAVE THOUGHT POSSIBLE.

POW

ROURKE WANTED TO GET RID OF MILO ONCE AND FOR ALL.

SAY GOODNIGHT, GRACIE.

MILO GRABBED A PIECE OF SHATTERED GLASS FROM KIDA'S POD AND CUT ROURKE.

YYAAAH!

WOW.

THE POWER OF ATLANTIS MADE ROURKE TURN TO STONE.

THE VEHICLE SHATTERED, AND MILO PLUMMETED TO THE GROUND.

ROURKE WAS FINISHED!

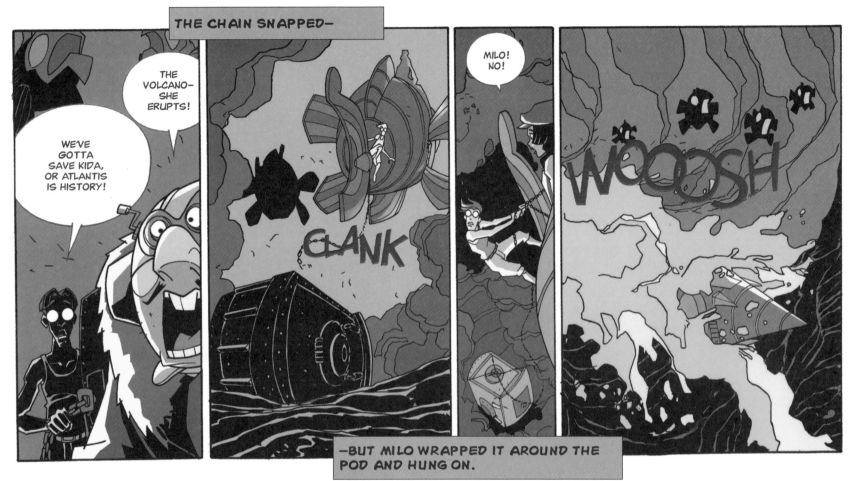

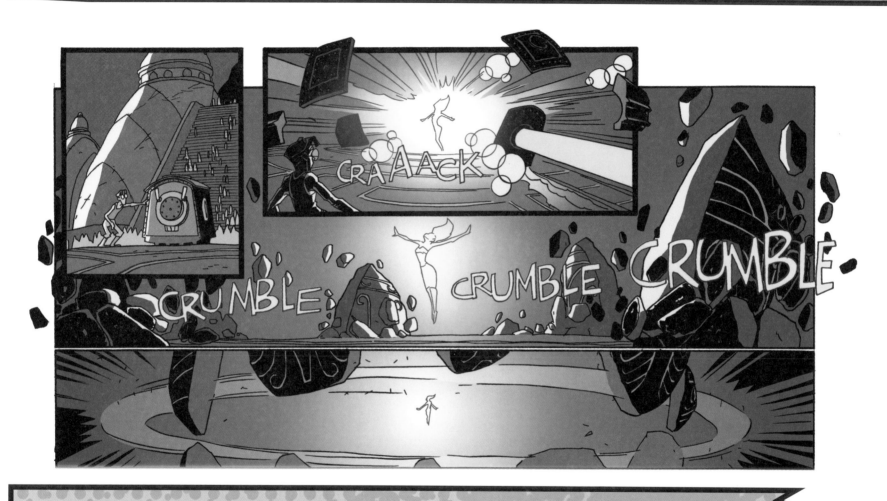

STUNNED, MILO COULD ONLY STAND AND WATCH AS KIDA ASCENDED HIGH ABOVE THE CITY. THE STONES ROSE TO MEET HER AND BEGAN TO ORBIT ONCE MORE.

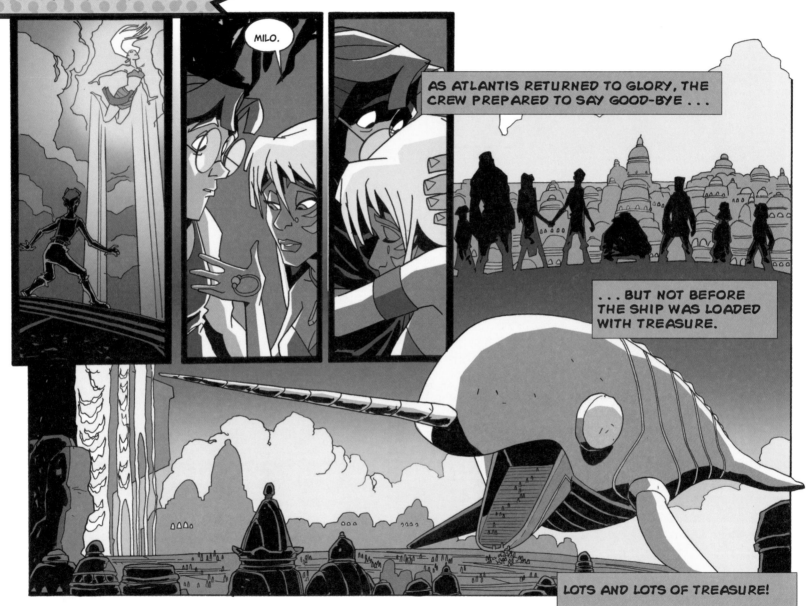

NO! KIDA WAS SAFE!

MILO.

AS ATLANTIS RETURNED TO GLORY, THE CREW PREPARED TO SAY GOOD-BYE . . .

. . . BUT NOT BEFORE THE SHIP WAS LOADED WITH TREASURE.

LOTS AND LOTS OF TREASURE!